The Midas Touch

Welcome to the World of Mythology

Mythology gives interesting explanations about many tribulations in life and tries to satisfy your curiosity. Many stories have been created to explain surprising or frightening phenomena. Thus, different countries and peoples throughout the world have their own myths.

Greek and Roman mythology is deeply loved, because it is a treasury of imagination that weaves together the exciting legends of surreal gods, heroines, and heroes. As a mirror that reflects the human world, Greek and Roman mythology is recommended as a must-read in order to understand western culture and thinking.

Although the basis of these classical stories can be traced back as far as the prehistoric age, what is it in these myths that can still enchant you, a citizen of the contemporary world? The secret is that mythology transcends time and

space and keeps intact the internal desires of human beings. The exciting adventures allow you unlimited access to the important aspects of life: war and peace, life and death, good and evil, and love and hatred.

The Olympian gods who appear in Greek and Roman mythology are not always described as perfect, omnipotent gods. As these gods fight in anger, trick other gods, and suffer the pain of love and jealousy, they often resemble humans. In Let's Enjoy Mythology, the second volume in the series Reading Greek and Roman Mythology in English, you can encounter many heroes, heroines, gods, and goddesses with very human characteristics.

Reading Greek and Roman Mythology in English will guide you through your journey into the imaginary world of the ancient Greeks. Your trip will be to a place that transcends time and space.

The characters in the stories

King Midas

He was once a very rich king who ruled the land of Phygia. Midas took good care of Silenus who was a mentor of Dionysus. In return, Dionysus told King Midas that he would grant any wish that he made. Midas asked that everything he touched would be turned into gold.

Dionysus

He was known as Bacchus in Roman mythology. Dionysus was the god of wine and ecstasy, and liberation and freedom. He was the son of Zeus and Semele. Owing to Hera's jealousy, Dionysus grew in the thigh of Zeus, until he was born. Dionysus was raised by nymphs. As an adult, he wandered in various countries. Mythology has it that Hera was the one who implanted craziness in him.

Silenus

He was a satyr. Silenus is described as an old drunk with a thick beard. He had legs and a tale of a horse. The mythology has it that anyone who would touch him could extract wisdom from him, as he was a very wise satyr. Silenus was a mentor and companion of Dionysus, the god of wine.

Daedalus

His name means "master-hand." Daedalus was the best inventor in Athens. He built the Labyrinth, a huge maze to confine the Minotaur. King Minos, who accused Daedalus of helping Theseus, locked Daedalus in a tower. To escape, Daedalus built wings for himself and his son Icarus.

Icarus

He was the son of Daedalus. To escape from the tower where he was locked up with his father, Icarus flew in the sky, wearing the wings made by his father. However, he fell into the sea and drowned, because he ignored his father's warning and had flown too close to the sun. The sun's heat had melted the wax by which his wings were fastened.

Pygmalion

He was a famous sculptor on Cyprus Island. Pygmalion created a statue of a beautiful maiden and fell in love with the statue. As he prayed to Aphrodite to meet a woman exactly like his statue, the goddess brought the statue to life.

Galatea

She was a statue of a beautiful maiden that Pygmalion carved by using his whole heart and soul. The legend has it that in order to carve a statue of the most beautiful woman, Pygmalion's passion created the statue to represent a lovely and mythical water nymph. The statue was given life by Aphrodite after Pygmalion fell in love with it.

Before Reading *The Midas Touch*

In this book, there are several interesting stories, including the Midas Touch, the Flight of Daedalus and Icarus, and Pygmalion and Galatea.

King Midas was the envy of everyone in the world. He had it all, especially, fame and fortune. However, he wanted more. Dionysus, the god of wine, granted Midas a wish for treating Silenus hospitably. Midas asked Dionysus to give him the ability to turn all he touched into gold. Do you think King Midas became richer after he realized his wish to make everything become gold?

Daedalus, the most ingenious inventor in Athens, was so jealous of his nephew who surpassed him in talent that he tossed the boy from the top of a castle. Daedalus was banished from Athens and fled to Crete, which was ruled by King Minos.

However, he hadn't been punished enough. He ended up being locked in a tall tower with his beloved son, Icarus, after King Minos suspected Daedalus of treachery. What do you think happened next to Daedalus and Icarus?

Pygmalion was a gifted artist. He had no interest in the women around him. All day long, he concentrated on his art, carving his favorite figures, until one day he carved a statue of a beautiful woman. The statue was so perfect that everyone thought it was a real woman. Just by looking at the statue every day, Pygmalion fell in love with her. He even gave the statue a name: Galatea. What would happen to Pygmalion and his love for the statue of a maiden?

Contents

The Midas
Touch

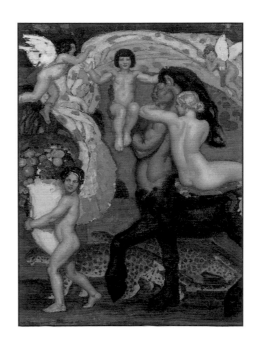

I n the land of Phrygia, there was a King
named Midas.

He was a good king.

He was fair and his people loved him.

But he had one fault.

He often spoke before thinking.

So he sometimes made people upset.

And sometimes he made trouble for himself.

Midas enjoyed nature.

He had large gardens at his palace.

One day, the servants found a man sleeping in King's gardens.

King Midas didn't like strange people in his gardens. He worried that strangers would hurt his flowers.

The servants took the man to King Midas.

The king was not happy with the old man
at first. But then King Midas recognized
the old man.

"You are Selinus, aren't you?" asked the king.

The old man looked as if he drank too much
wine last night. Leaves and twigs were in
his hair.

He answered, "Yes, I am Selinus. I got lost.
I think I drank too much wine."

Selinus was actually one of the Satyrs.

Satyrs were famous for getting drunk and chasing women. This made them tired. So Satyrs usually slept during the day.

Selinus was also the teacher of Dionysus, the god of wine. After Dionysus grew up, Selinus and many other Satyrs served him.

Satyrs Enjoying a Feast

"Welcome!" said King Midas, "any friend of
Dionysus is a friend of mine."
King Midas invited Selinus to stay in his
palace.
The king and Selinus ate, drank,
and sang for ten days and ten nights.
They both liked food and wine very much.
Selinus told many stories about the young
god, Dionysus.

At the end of ten days, a messenger came
to King Midas. Dionysus had sent this man.
The messenger told the king that Dionysus
was nearby.
The god of wine wanted to see Selinus.
So King Midas and Selinus made a journey
to see Dionysus.

Soon, King Midas entered the camp of
Dionysus with Selinus.

The god was happy to see his old teacher.

"My old friend, where did you go?"
Dionysus asked.

"We were looking everywhere for you.

Then we heard you were with
King Midas.

Tell me, teacher, how did
the king treat you?"

Selinus smiled as
he replied.

"Like royalty,
my lord.

He gave me a feast
like I have never
seen before.

We ate, drank,
and sang songs
about you."

Dionysus wanted to reward King Midas.
He said, "Dear king, you have a good heart.
I want to give you a gift.
Ask me for anything you wish.
If I can give it to you, I will."
King Midas did not think long.
Immediately he said,
"I wish that everything I touch
turns to gold."
The king did not love only
gardens, food, and wine,
but he also loved wealth.

Dionysus was not happy.

He looked at King Midas carefully.

"Are you sure that is what you want?

Maybe you should think some more."

"My lord, please do not be angry," said

King Midas.

"But that is what I want more than anything

else."

"Then you shall have it," said Dionysus.

King Midas was very
excited as he returned
home.
On the way, he decided
to test his new power.
The king saw a small branch
on an oak tree. He reached up
and broke it off.
Instantly, it turned to gold.
The king was even more excited.
He picked up a stone. It changed to gold as
soon as he touched it.

Then the king saw
an apple. He picked
it off the branch.
The apple changed
to gold instantly.

King Midas was very happy.
He hurried home and went to his favorite
roses. One by one, he turned them into gold.
He jumped for joy. Then he ordered his
servants to make a meal.

When the food was ready, the king sat down
with his daughter.
The king was very hungry.
But when he touched a piece of bread,
it became hard and heavy gold. With a fork,
he picked up a piece of meat and he put it in
his mouth. The meat instantly changed into
gold. He almost broke his tooth!

King Midas grabbed a cup of wine.
The cup was already gold,
so there was no change.
The king poured the wine into his mouth.
It instantly turned to gold.

King Midas started to choke.

He stood up and grabbed his chest.

His daughter stood up too and came near him.

The king spit out the gold.

He grabbed his daughter's arm for support.

Then he saw something terrible.

His daughter, once warm and living,

was now cold and dead!

She was a perfect statue in solid gold.

He felt horrible. He had killed his daughter!

King Midas also realized that he couldn't
eat or drink.
He yelled at his servants.
"We're going back to see Dionysus!"
The servants ran around to prepare for the
trip. But they did not come near their king.

05

The next day, King Midas came running into Dionysus's camp.
King Midas threw himself at Dionysus's feet.
"Please take this power away from me," pleaded King Midas.
"It is not good, it is very terrible!
I have killed my daughter!
I will starve to death!"

"Very well then," said Dionysus.
"You have learned your lesson. There are more important things in life than wealth.
You must go to the river Pactolus.
There you will find a spring.
Take a bath in this spring. The waters will take away your foolish power."

Dionysus

King Midas ran a long way to this river.
As soon as he found the spring, the king
jumped in. The river carried his golden
touch away.

But the power did not completely disappear.
It went far down the river. There, along the
sides of the river was a lot of sand.

All of this sand turned to gold!

This part of the river
was in the kingdom of Lydia.
Because of King Midas,
Lydia became rich!
It was the richest kingdom
of the ancient world.
Gold coins were first used as money
in Lydia.

King Midas returned to his palace.
But his daughter was still dead.
The king was ashamed and sad.
He decided to forget about wealth.
He went to live in the forest. He became a
follower of Pan, the god of nature.
King Midas left his palace and his gold
forever.

Daedalus and
the Flight of Icarus

D aedalus was a very clever man.
He was the smartest inventor in
Greece.
He was a member of the royal family in
Athens.

Daedalus was very proud of his inventions.
His sister asked him to teach her son, Perdix.
Daedalus taught his nephew many things.
Perdix was a good student. He learned
quickly.

One day,
Perdix was walking
on the beach.
He found a fish spine.
He made a copy of the
spine using metal. Perdix
found that his metal
copy cut wood easily.
He had invented
the saw!

Next, Perdix took two
small pieces of metal.

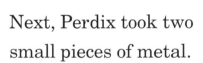

He made one end of each
sharp. Then he joined the
other two ends together.
This tool was used to
draw perfect circles.
It is now called
'compasses'.

Many people liked Perdix's inventions.
But Daedalus became jealous of him.
One day, Daedalus called to Perdix.
"Perdix, today I want to explain wind to
you."
They climbed to the top of the Acropolis.
Daedalus told his nephew to walk to the
edge.
"The wind's power is strong over there,"
explained Daedalus.
When Perdix moved to the edge of the roof,
Daedalus pushed Perdix!

Perdix fell from the roof.
Athena, the goddess of
wisdom and intelligence,
saw Perdix falling.
She felt sorry for Perdix.
Athena turned Perdix into
a bird.

People called this new bird
the Partridge.
This bird does not make
nests in high places.
It remembers the fall of the first partridge,
Perdix. So it makes nests in low places near
the ground.

Daedalus did not escape punishment. Some people saw him push Perdix off the roof. So the townsfolk judged Daedalus. Because he was in the royal family, he was not killed. Instead, he was told to leave and never come back.

Daedalus went to Crete. Minos was the king there.

Daedalus was famous, so King Minos knew about him. He hired Daedalus immediately. Daedalus made the Labyrinth for King Minos. King Minos kept the Minotaur in this giant maze. Every nine year, 14 Athenians were sent to Crete. The Minotaur would eat them.

34

One year, Theseus, a hero of Athens came
to kill the Minotaur.
King Minos's daughter, Ariadne,
fell in love with Theseus.
She gave Theseus a ball of string that
could help him to find the way out easily.
Theseus went into the Labyrinth and killed
the Minotaur.
Then he escaped from Crete with Ariadne.

© Photo RMN - R.G. Ojeda / GNC media, Seoul 2003

Theseus and Ariadne

King Minos was very angry.
He thought that Daedalus had helped
Theseus. So King Minos locked the inventor
and also his son, Icarus in a high tower.
Daedalus could have easily escaped the tower.
But he did not know how to get off the island
of Crete.
King Minos's soldiers guarded the boats.
Everyone who left the island was searched
carefully.

One day, Daedalus had a good idea.
'King Minos controls the land and the sea,'
thought Daedalus, 'but he does not control
the sky. So my son and I must escape through
the air.'
Daedalus had a very clever idea. He would
make two pairs of wings. One would be for
him and the other set would be for Icarus.
They could fly far away from Crete!

Daedalus planned
to fly to Sicily.
The king there
was wise and good.
In Sicily,
they would be
safe from
King Minos.

So Daedalus began to make the wings.

He collected feathers from birds.

He also collected wax from candles.

He tied the feathers together with thread.

For the smaller feathers, he used the wax.

He worked hard, day and night.

Sometimes Icarus helped his father collect feathers.

Finally, Daedalus finished one large pair of
wings. Daedalus had to test them before he
made another set for Icarus.
He tied them to his arms. Then he waved
his arms up and down quickly.
He flew up into the air!
If he waved his arms very fast,
he went up.
If he spread his
arms wide,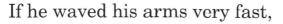
he came down slowly.
His wings worked!
Daedalus quickly made
another pair of wings.

On a clear day, it was time to escape.
Daedalus put the wings on Icarus.
Then Daedalus put on his own wings.
He told Icarus to be careful.

"Dear son, stay near me," he said.
"Do not fly too low!
There is water in the air near the ocean.
It will make your wings too heavy."

"Do not fly too high!
The sun will melt the wax and the small
feathers will fall off.
Then you will fall from the sky.
Stay in the cool, dry air between the ocean
and the sun. That is where I will fly.
Stay near me! Let's fly!"
As Daedalus spoke
to Icarus, his hands
shook. He knew
flying was dangerous.

🔘 09 Daedalus tested the wind.

Then he waved his arms strongly.

He rose into the air.

He shouted back to Icarus.

"Follow me, my son!"

Icarus was very excited.

He quickly followed his father.

He jumped in the air and waved his arms.

He was flying!

Together, father and son flew away from
the tower.

42

The flight started well.

Sicily was far to the west.

Daedalus saw the sun rising in the east.
He flew away from it. Soon, Daedalus and
Icarus passed the islands of Delos and Samos.
Daedalus checked on his son often.
They continued to the west.
But the sun climbed to the middle of the sky.
Daedalus could no longer fly away from the
sun. So he looked closely at the ocean and
the islands.

Icarus was having a lot of fun!
Sometimes he looked at the waves far below.
Sometimes he saw dolphins jumping.
At other times, he saw big turtles come up
for air.
Then Icarus became tired of looking down.
He looked up at the clouds.
They seemed very near.

He wanted to fly into them.

Their shapes were fantastic!

Soon he started to fly higher and higher.

He flew to the right, and to the left.

He forgot his father's warning.

The clouds were cold and dark.

So Icarus flew above the clouds.

The sun was warm there.

The sun started to melt the wax on Icarus's
wings. But the boy did not notice.
He flew higher and higher.
He liked the warmth of the sun.
Soon, all the wax on his wings melted.
Feathers started to fall from his wings.

Suddenly, Icarus was
afraid. But it was too
late.
Holes appeared in
his wings.
He started to fall.
He waved his arms
harder. Still he fell.
He waved his arms
even harder. But it
didn't help.
He was falling very
quickly!
He cried out to his
father and
fell into the sea.
Daedalus did not see
his son flying near the
sun. But he heard Icarus
call out.

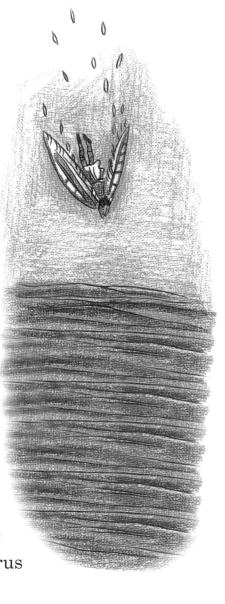

Daedalus turned around. But he could not
see where his son went.

He looked left and right. He looked up and
down. But he could not find Icarus.

Daedalus shouted, "Icarus, where are you?
Where are you?"

But there was no answer.

Suddenly, Daedalus saw feathers on the
water. He put his arms next to his body.
Daedalus fell from the sky like a stone.
He dove into the water.
There he found Icarus.
His son was just under the water.
Icarus was not moving.

There was a small island nearby.
Daedalus grabbed Icarus.
He pulled his son to the island.
But it was too late. Icarus was dead.
Daedalus held his son's body for a long time.
He cried very much.
Then he buried his son on the island.

The land where Icarus was buried is now called 'Icaria'.
The ocean where Icarus fell is now called the 'Icarian Sea'.

Pygmalion and Galatea

Pygmalion was a very good artist.

He lived on the island of Cyprus.

He made beautiful statues.

Pygmalion loved his work.

He would spend all day making shapes
from rock and wood.

He was very busy,
so he didn't have many friends.

Pygmalion's parents wanted him to marry.
He was both talented and handsome.
It would be easy for him to find a wife.
But Pygmalion thought the women on
Cyprus were silly. He promised himself he
would never marry.
So Pygmalion spent all his time working.
He made shapes of men, women, children,
and animals. His favorite material was ivory.

One day, he saw a really big piece of ivory.

He bought it and took it home.

He spent many days working on it.

Sometimes he worked all night!

Finally he created a beautiful statue.

It was in the shape of a woman.

This statue was the best he ever made.

Pygmalion's statue became famous.

It was so good,

people thought it was a real woman!

But other women did not like the statue.

It was so beautiful that they were jealous

of it.

The statue had perfect white skin.

The face was like a goddess.

Pygmalion was proud of his work.

Galatea Statue

He would spend hours just looking at it.
He would put his hand on its arm or on its
face. Sometimes even he could not believe
it was not a real woman!

Pygmalion and Galatea

12 Soon, Pygmalion thought only about his
statue. He fell in love with it!

Pygmalion made a name for it.

He called it 'Galatea'.

This means 'sleeping love' in Greek.

Pygmalion made little birds and flowers
out of ivory. He put these around Galatea's
feet. He gave the statue a necklace and put
rings on her fingers.

Pygmalion even put clothes on the statue!

At night, he put Galatea on a bed.

He put a soft pillow under her head.

He kissed her before he went to sleep.

Her skin looked real.

It had a pale white glow.

But she was cold and hard to his touch.

She was, after all, just ivory.

Every year, there was a festival on Cyprus.
This festival was for Aphrodite, the goddess
of beauty and love.

People visited Aphrodite's temples. They
gave gifts to the goddess. They prayed that
they would find true love.

Pygmalion liked Aphrodite.
Every year, he went to her temple. He brought
the goddess many small beautiful statues.

13

This year, he did the same.

But this time, his prayers were different.

"Great Aphrodite, please hear me," he prayed, "the gods can do anything. Please give me a wife."

Pygmalion wanted to say, "Change Galatea into my wife." But Pygmalion was not so bold. Instead he said, "Give me a wife like Galatea."

Aphrodite heard Pygmalion's prayer.
She was impressed by his words.
He seemed so sincere and excited.

While Pygmalion was still praying,
Aphrodite went to his house.
There she saw the ivory statue, Galatea.
Even she was amazed because it looked so
real.

In Aphrodite's temple, Pygmalion was still
praying. Suddenly the flame of the candle
grew bigger and then became small again.
Pygmalion was amazed.
The flame became large two more times.
All the people in the temple were very exited.
Someone's prayers were answered!
Pygmalion was also excited.
He had a good feeling in his heart.
He hurried home.

14 At night, before sleeping, he kissed Galatea
as usual. But what was this?
Galatea's lips were not cold and hard.
They were soft and warm!
He put his hand on the statue's arm.
He could not believe it! The skin was warm!
There was blood under the skin!
At first Pygmalion could not speak.
Then he said softly, "Thank you, Aphrodite.
Thank you!"

He kissed the statue once more.

But it was not a statue anymore.

The lips were ruby red.

The eyes opened. They were deep blue.

Galatea had become alive!

When Galatea opened her eyes,

she fell in love with Pygmalion.

They made plans for a wedding.

Aphrodite married Pygmalion and
Galatea in her temple.

Pygmalion and Galatea
wanted to thank Aphrodite.
Every year, they brought many gifts
to her temple.
Aphrodite gave them long and
happy lives in return.
Pygmalion and Galatea had two
daughters, Pahphos and Metharme.

A new city on Cyprus was named
after Pahphos.
The city became the center
for honoring Aphrodite.

Reading Comprehension

○ Read and answer the questions.

▸ **The Midas Touch**

1. What was King Midas's fault?

    (A) He loved gold more than his family.
    (B) He ate too much and became too fat.
    (C) He didn't think before he spoke.
    (D) He didn't have any sons.

2. What was the relationship between Selinus and Dionysus?

    (A) Selinus had been Dionysus's teacher.
    (B) Selinus was the father of Dionysus.
    (C) Dionysus was a fellow Satyr.
    (D) Dionysus was Selinus's uncle.

3. What was the first thing that King Midas turned to gold?

    (A) an apple
    (B) a twig
    (C) a stone
    (D) his roses

4. What did King Midas say to Dionysus after he had turned his daughter into gold?

   (A) "My lord, please do not be angry."
   (B) "I wish that everything I touch turns to gold."
   (C) "Please take my power away from me."
   (D) "There are more improtant things in life than wealth."

5. Where did King Midas have to go to get rid of his power?

   (A) his rose garden
   (B) the river Pactolus
   (C) the Kingdom of Lydia
   (D) the forest

6. What did King Midas have to do in the spring?

   (A) wash his hair
   (B) swim
   (C) drink water
   (D) take a bath

▶ Daedalus and the Flight of Icarus

1. What is the relationship between Daedalus and Perdix?

    (A) uncle and nephew
    (B) father and son
    (C) brothers
    (D) master and slave

2. Who invented the saw? _____

3. What's the name of the bird which Perdix turned into?

    _____

4. Why did Daedalus leave Athens?

    (A) Because he wanted to work for King
        Minos.
    (B) Because he had to escape to Sicily where
        he would be safe.
    (C) Because he was convicted of killing
        Perdix.
    (D) Because his family was in Sicily.

5. Why did King Minos lock up Daedalus and Icarus?

   (A) Because he was angry at all Athenians.
   (B) Because he thought Daedalus had helped a hero from Athens.
   (C) Because he thought Daedalus had killed the Minotaur.
   (D) Because he hated Daedalus and Icarus.

6. Chose all the materials Daedalus used to make the wings.

   (A) glue
   (B) wax
   (C) feathers
   (D) cloth

7. How did Icarus die?

   _____

   _____

   _____

▶ Pygmalion and Galatea

1. What did Pygmalion do for a living?

   _____

2. Write True(T) or False(F).

   _____ Pygmalion didn't like women
            because they were not beautiful.

   _____ Aphrodite conducted the marriage
            ceremony between Pygmalion and
            Galatea.

3. What was Galatea created out of?

   (A) wood
   (B) marble
   (C) ivory
   (D) flesh and bone

4. How did Aphrodite signal her answer to
   Pygmalion?

   (A) She told him his future through an oracle.
   (B) She came to him in a dream.
   (C) She made a flame in her temple grow three
       times.
   (D) She sent her messenger.

● Read and talk about it.

. . . Soon, King Midas entered the camp of Dionysus with Selinus. The god was happy to see his old teacher.

"My old friend, where did you go?" Dionysus asked.

"We were looking everywhere for you. Then we heard you were with King Midas.

Tell me, teacher, how did the king treat you?"

Selinus smiled as he replied.

"Like royalty, my lord. He gave me a feast like I have never seen before. We ate, drank, and sang songs about you."

Dionysus wanted to reward King Midas.

He said, "Dear king, you have a good heart.

I want to give you a gift. Ask me for anything you wish.

If I can give it to you, I will." . . .

1. Dionysus gave King Midas the 'golden touch', which became a curse for Midas.
   What would you have wished for if you were Midas?

   _____

   _____

   _____

. . . Icarus was having a lot of fun!
Sometimes he looked at the waves far below.
Sometimes he saw dolphins jumping.
At other times, he saw big turtles come up for air.
Then Icarus became tired of looking down.
He looked up at the clouds.
They seemed very near.
He wanted to fly into them.
Their shapes were fantastic!
Soon he started to fly higher and higher.
He flew to the right, and to the left.
He forgot his father's warning.
The clouds were cold and dark.
So Icarus flew above the clouds.
The sun was warm there. . . .

2. What would you want to look at if you could
   fly like Icarus?

_____

_____

_____

. . . Soon, Pygmalion thought only about his statue.

He fell in love with it!

Pygmalion made a name for it.

He called it 'Galatea'.

This means 'sleeping love' in Greek.

Pygmalion made little birds and flowers out of ivory.

He put these around Galatea's feet.

He gave the statue a necklace and put rings on her fingers.

Pygmalion even put clothes on the statue!

At night, he put Galatea on a bed.

He put a soft pillow under her head.

He kissed her before he went to sleep.

Her skin looked real.

It had a pale white glow. . . .

3. What would you have made or done for Galatea if you were Pygmalion?

_____

_____

_____

The Signs of the Zodiac

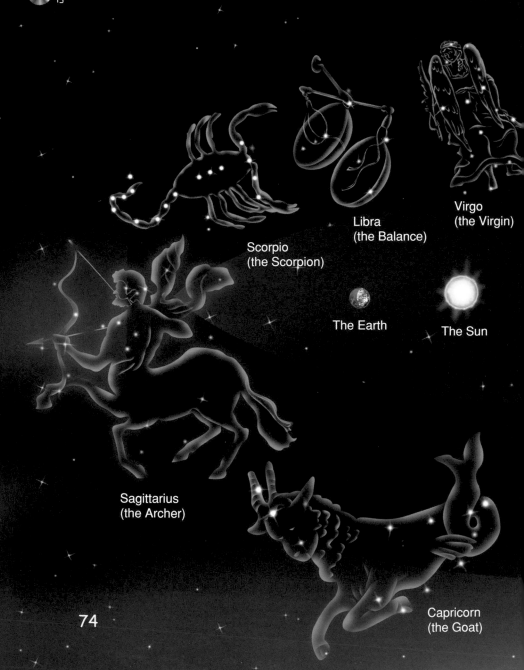

15

Scorpio
(the Scorpion)

Libra
(the Balance)

Virgo
(the Virgin)

The Earth

The Sun

Sagittarius
(the Archer)

Capricorn
(the Goat)

The word "zodiac" comes from a Greek word meaning, "the circle of animals".
Where did the zodiac come from?
In this section, you can find the Greek Myths that explain the origins of these signs.

Leo
(the Lion)

Cancer
(the Crab)

Gemini
(the Twins)

Taurus
(the Bull)

Aries
(the Ram)

Pisces
(the Fishes)

Aquarius
(the Water Bearer)

Aries (the Ram)

March 21st ~ April 20th

The origin of Aries stems from the Tale of the Golden Ram. The ram safely carried off Phrixus. Phrixus sacrificed the Golden Ram to Zeus and in turn, Zeus placed the ram in the heavens.

Taurus (the Bull)

April 21st ~ May 20th

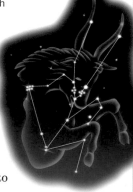

The origin of Taurus stems from the Tale of Europa and the Bull. Zeus turned himself into a bull in order to attract Europa to him.

The bull carried Europa across the sea to Crete.

In remembrance, Zeus placed the image of the bull in the stars.

Gemini (the Twins)

May 21st ~ June 21st

This sign stems from the Tale of Castor and Pollux. Castor and Pollux were twins. They both loved each other very much. In honor of the brothers's great love, Zeus placed them among the stars.

Cancer (the Crab)

June 22nd ~ July 22nd

The sign of Cancer stems from one of the 12 Labors of Hercules.

Hera sent the crab to kill Hercules. But Hercules crushed the crab under his foot just before he defeated the Hydra. To honor the crab, Hera placed it among the stars.

Leo (the Lion)
July 23rd ~ August 22nd

The sign of Leo stems
from another of
Hercules 12 Labors. Hercules's
first labor was to kill a lion that lived
in Nemea valley. He killed the
Nemea lion with his hands.
In remembrance of the grand battle,
Zeus placed the Lion of Nemea
among the stars.

Libra (the Balance)
September 23rd ~ October 21st

The Libra are the scales that balance
justice. They are held
by the goddess of
divine justice,
Themis. Libra
shines right beside
Virgo which
represents Astraea,
daughter of Themis.

Virgo (the Virgin)
August 23rd ~ September 22nd

Virgo's origin stems from the Tale of
Pandora. Virgo represents the
goddess of purity and innocence,
Astraea. After Pandora opened the

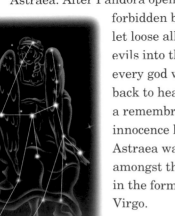

forbidden box and
let loose all the
evils into the world,
every god went
back to heaven. As
a remembrance of
innocence lost,
Astraea was placed
amongst the stars
in the form of
Virgo.

Scorpio (the Scorpion)
October 22nd ~ November 21st

The sign of Scorpio stems from the
Tale of Orion. Orion and Artemis
were great hunting partners, which
made Artemis's brother Apollo very
jealous. Apollo pleaded with Gaea to
kill Orion. So Gaea created the
scorpion and killed great Orion. In
remembrance of this act, Zeus placed
Orion and the scorpion amongst the
stars. But they never
appear at the
same time.

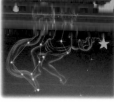

Sagittarius (the Archer)
November 23rd ~ December 21st

This sign is representative of Cheiron. Cheiron was the friend of many great heroes in Greek mythology such as Achilles and Hercules. Hercules accidentally shot Cheiron in the leg with a poison arrow. Cheiron was immortal so he couldn't die. Instead, he had to endure the unending pain. Cheiron begged Zeus to kill him. To honor Cheiron, Zeus placed him among the stars.

 19

Capricorn (the Goat)
December 22nd ~ January 19th

The sign of Capricorn represents the goat Amalthea who fed the infant Zeus. It's said that Zeus placed her among the stars in gratitude.

Aquarius
(the Water Bearer)
January 20th ~ February 18th

The sign of Aquarius stems from the Tale of Deucalion's Flood. In this tale, Zeus pours all the waters of the heavens onto earth to wash away all the evil creatures. Deucalion and his wife Pyrrha were the only survivors of the great flood.

Pisces (the Fishes)
February 19th ~ March 20th

The Pisces represents the goddess of love & beauty, Aphrodite and her son the god of love, Eros. They were taking a stroll down the Euphrates River when there was a typhoon. They pleaded for Zeus to help them escape, so Zeus changed them into fish and they swam away safely. In remembrance of this, Aphrodite is the big fish constellation and Eros is the small fish constellation.

希臘羅馬神話故事 ⑪

點石成金 The Midas Touch

First Published May, 2011
First Printing May, 2011

Original Story by Thomas Bulfinch
Rewritten by Brian Stuart
Illustrated by Ludmila Pipchenko
Designer by Eonju No
Translated by Jia-chen Chuo

Printed and distributed by Cosmos Culture Ltd.
Tel: 02-2365-9739
Fax: 02-2365-9835
http://www.icosmos.com.tw
Publisher: Value-Deliver Culture Ltd.

The Midas Touch

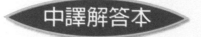

中譯解答本

卓加真　譯

神話以趣味的方式，為我們生活中的煩惱提出解釋，並滿足我們的好奇心。許多故事的編寫，都是為了解釋一些令人驚奇或恐懼的現象，因此，世界各地不同的國家、民族，都有屬於自己的神話。

希臘與羅馬神話充滿想像力，並結合了諸神與英雄們激盪人心的傳奇故事，因此特別為人所津津樂道。希臘與羅馬神話反應了真實的人類世界，因此，閱讀神話對於瞭解西方文化與思維，有極大的幫助。

這些經典故事的背景，可追溯至史前時代，但對於當代的讀者而言，它們深具魅力的法寶何在？其秘密就在於，神話能超越時空，完整地呈現人類心中的慾望。這些激盪人心的冒險故事，將帶您經歷生命中的各種重要事件：戰爭與和平、生命與死亡、善與惡，以及各種愛恨情仇。

希臘與羅馬神話裡所描繪的諸神，並不全是完美、萬能的天神，他們和人類一樣，會因憤怒而打鬥，會耍詭計戲弄其他天神，會因愛與嫉妒而感到痛苦。在 Let's Enjoy Mythology 系列的第二部 Reading Greek and Roman Mythology in English 中，你將會讀到許多具有人類特質的英雄、女英雄、眾神和女神的故事。

Reading Greek and Roman Mythology in English 將引領你穿越時空，一探想像中的古希臘世界。

前言

在本書裡頭，講了三個有趣的故事：〈點石成金的麥達斯〉、〈父子逃亡記〉和〈美夢成真〉。

麥達斯國王的富貴和聲譽，令世人無不欣羨，但他卻不知足。因為他曾熱誠招待過席萊納斯，酒神戴歐尼修斯就答應他，願意幫他實現他的一個願望。他便請戴歐尼修斯賜給他點石成金的能力。當他體會到點石成金究竟是什麼樣的一種願望時，你想，他變得更加富裕了？

戴達勒斯是雅典城首屈一指的發明天才，但他妒忌青出於藍的姪子，便將姪子從城堡上推落致死。雅典城人民因此驅逐了他，他逃到由麥諾斯國王所統治的克里特島。然而，他所受的懲罰並未結束。麥諾斯國王懷疑他謀反，最後他就和愛子伊卡魯斯一起被監禁在一座高塔上。你想，他們這對父子接著會如何？

皮葛馬連是一個很有天賦的藝術家。他對身旁圍繞的女子毫無興趣，成天只是全神貫注地做著他的創作，雕刻他自己喜歡的東西。有一天，他雕了一個美麗女性的雕像，雕像栩栩如生，簡直和真人沒有兩樣。他每天就楞楞地凝視著這個雕像，最後，他竟愛上了雕像，還幫它取了名字「葛拉蒂」。

他，還有他對雕像女子的愛意，這故事會如何地發展下去呢？

目錄

點石成金的麥達斯

p. 10

在福萊吉亞國度，
有位國王，名爲麥達斯。
他是一位賢明的君主，
爲人公正，受民愛戴。
他唯一的缺點，
是快人快語，不經思考。
常因此得罪人，
甚至爲自己惹禍上身。

- **Phrygia**
  福萊吉亞國
- **fair** [fer]
  公平的；公正的
- **fault** [fɔːlt] 缺點
- **upset** [ʌp`set]
  心煩的；苦惱的
- **make trouble**
  [meɪk `trʌble] 惹麻煩

-----

p. 11

麥達斯喜愛大自然，
他在宮殿中開闢了大片的花園。
有一天，
僕人發現有人睡在國王的花園裡。
國王不喜歡讓外人進入花園，
擔心花園會遭到破壞。
僕人將陌生人帶到國王面前。

- **enjoy** [ɪn`dʒɔɪ]
  享受；喜愛
- **servant** [`sɜːrvənt]
  僕人；佣人
- **sleep** [sliːp] 睡覺
- **worry** [`wɜːri]
  擔心；憂慮
- **stranger** [`streɪndʒə(r)]
  陌生人
- **hurt** [hɜːrt] 損害；危害
- **take . . . to . . .**
  帶……去……

p. 12

起初，國王對這老人極為不悅，
但沒多久，國王認出這個人。
「你是席萊納斯，對吧？」
國王問道。
老人一副宿醉模樣，
像是昨晚喝了太多酒一樣，
髮上還插了樹枝和樹葉。
老人回答道：
「沒錯，我就是席萊納斯，
我喝多了酒，迷路了。」
席萊納斯其實是一位牧神。

- **then** [ðen] 之後
- **Selinus** 席萊納斯
- **as if** [əz ɪf]
  猶如；好似
- **last night** [læst naɪt]
  前一晚
- **wine** [waɪn] 葡萄酒
- **twig** [twɪg]
  細枝；嫩葉

p. 13

牧神是出了名的愛喝酒，
而且很喜歡追逐女性，
把自己弄得精疲力竭，
因此常常可以看到他們白天裡在睡覺。
席萊納斯也是酒神戴歐尼修斯的老師。
等酒神長大後，
席萊納斯就和其他牧神一起服侍酒神。
〔圖〕牧神享用美食

- **famous for** [ˋfeɪməs fə(r)]
  以……為名
- **get drunk** [get drʌŋk]
  使酒醉的
  （drunk是drink的過去式）
- **chase** [tʃeɪs] 追逐；追尋
- **tired** [ˋtaɪərd] 疲倦的
- **usually** [ˋjuːʒʊəli]
  通常地；慣常地
- **during the day**
  [ˋdʊrɪŋ ðə deɪ] 在白天裡
- **grew up** [gruː ʌp] 長大
  （grew是grow的過去式）
- **serve** [sɜːrv] 服侍

---

p. 14

「歡迎！」國王說道：
「酒神的朋友，就是我的朋友。」
國王麥達斯邀請席萊納斯在皇宮作客。
他們都熱愛美食和美酒，
兩人便大吃大喝，
歌唱歡樂了整整十天十夜，
席萊納斯還說了許多
酒神小時候的事情。

- **welcome** [ˋwelkəm] 歡迎
- **invite** [ɪnˋvaɪt] 邀請
- **stay in** [steɪ ɪn]
  停留在……
- **ate** [eɪt] 吃；喝
  （eat的過去式）
- **drank** [dræŋk] 飲；喝
  （drink的過去式）
- **sang** [sæŋ] 唱歌
  （sing的過去式）

p. 15

十天後，有位信差求見國王。

那是酒神的信差。

信差稟告國王說，

酒神就在附近，

想來看看席萊納斯。

因此國王便和席萊納斯一起去找酒神。

- **messenger** [ˋmesɪndʒə(r)]
  信差；送信人
- **nearby** [ˋnɪrbˌaɪ] 在附近
- **make a journey**
  [meɪk ə ˋdʒɜːrni]
  進行一趟旅行
- **journey** [ˋdʒɜːrni]
  旅行；行程

----

p. 16

沒多久，

兩人一起進入酒神的營帳裡。

酒神見到恩師，非常高興，

並問道：「老朋友，你去哪了呢？

我們到處在找你呀，

後來我們聽說你在國王麥達斯那裡。

告訴我，恩師，

國王待你如何？」

席萊納斯笑著回答：

「他待我如皇親國戚呢，主子。

他用山珍海味款待我，

- **camp** [kæmp]
  營地
- **look everywhere**
  [lʊk ˋevriwe(r)]
  到處找尋
- **treat** [triːt]
  款待

7

我們大吃大喝，
歌唱讚美你。」

- **royalty** [ˋrɔɪəltɪ]
  王族；皇族
- **lord** [lɔːrd] 統治者；
  閣下（尊稱）
- **feast** [fiːst] 筵席

---

p. 17

戴歐尼修斯想報答麥達斯國王，
便說：「敬愛的國王，
你真是心胸寬大，
我想送你一件禮物，
將你心中的願望告訴我，
我將盡力滿足你。」
國王毫不遲疑地回答：
「我希望只要是我碰過的東西，
都能夠變成黃金。」
國王不僅喜愛花園、食物、美酒，
也喜歡財富。

- **reward** [rɪˋwɔːrd]
  報答；報償
- **dear** [dɪr] 親愛的
- **wish** [wɪʃ]
- **immediately**
  [ɪˋmiːdɪətli]
  直接地；即刻地
- **not only . . . but also**
  [nɑːtˋoʊnli bʌtˋɔːlsoʊ]
  不僅……而且還

p. 18

戴歐尼修斯聽了悶悶不樂，
他猶豫地看著麥達斯國王。
「這真是你的願望嗎？
或許你該再仔細想一想。」
「天神，請別發怒，」國王說：
「但這的確是我的心願。」
酒神說：「那麼，你將如願以償。」

- **carefully** [ˋkɛrflɪ]
  小心謹慎地
- **sure** [ʃur] 確定的；
  有把握的
- **else** [ɛls] 其他；另外
- **shall** [ʃæl] 將；會

-----

p. 19

國王麥達斯非常興奮地回家了。
回家途中，他決定稍試身手。
國王看見橡樹上的一根小樹枝，
便伸手將它折下，
結果樹枝馬上變成黃金。
國王看了更加興奮，
他撿起一顆石頭，
石頭馬上就變成了黃金。
接著國王看見一顆蘋果。
他將蘋果從樹上摘下，
蘋果也變成了黃金。

- **on the way** [ɑ:n ðə wei]
  沿途中
- **oak tree** [ouk tri:]
  橡木樹
- **reach up** [ti:tʃ ʌp]
  向上伸手搆及
- **broke . . . off**
  [brouk ɔ:f] 折斷；折下
  （broke 是 break 的過去
  式）
- **instantly** [ˋɪnstəntli]
  立刻；馬上
- **even** [ˋi:vn] 甚至更；還
- **pick . . . off** [pɪk ɔ:f]
  摘下

9

p. 21

麥達斯國王非常地興奮。
他趕著回家，
來到他喜愛的玫瑰花前，
將一朵朵的玫瑰花變成黃金。
他雀躍不已，
接著命令僕人準備用餐。

用餐時刻，
國王與女兒一起準備用餐。
國王肚子很餓，
但是，當他伸手拿麵包時，
麵包就變成了硬梆梆的黃金。
他用叉子叉起肉片，
準備把它放進嘴裡時，
肉片也馬上變成黃金，
還差點讓他因而咬斷了牙齒！

麥達斯國王舉起酒杯，
酒杯是黃金做的，
因此沒有任何變化。
但當國王將酒倒入嘴裡時，
酒也馬上變成黃金。

- **hurry home**
  [ˋhɜːri houm] 趕緊回家
- **favorite** [ˋfeɪvərɪt]
  特別喜愛的
- **one by one** [wʌn baɪ wʌn] 一個接一個
- **jump for joy**
  [dʒʌmp fə(r) dʒɔɪ]
  因歡喜而跳躍
- **make a meal**
  [meɪk ə miːl] 準備膳食
- **a piece of** [ə piːs ʌv]
  一塊……
- **pick up** [pɪk ʌp] 挑選
- **put . . . in . . .** [put ɪn]
  放……進……
- **change into . . .**
  [tʃeɪndʒ ˋɪntə]
  轉變成……
- **grab** [græb] 抓取
- **a cup of wine**
  [ə kʌp ʌv waɪn] 一杯酒
- **pour** [pɔː(r)] 倒；灌

p. 22

國王被金塊給噎住，
他站起來揪著胸膛，
女兒隨之站起來走到他身邊，
國王將金塊吐出來，
他伸手抓住女兒的手，
把自己撐住。
接著，他目睹了一件可怕的事情：
他的女兒，
這曾是溫熱的血肉之軀，
此時竟變成得冰冷又無生息，
成為了結結實實黃金打造的雕像。
國王感到驚恐，
他竟殺了自己的女兒！

- **choke** [tʃouk]
  使窒息；哽住
- **near** [nɪr] 在……附近
- **spit out** [spɪt aut] 吐出
- **for support** [fə(r) sə`pɔːrt]
  藉以支撐
- **perfect** [`pɜːrfɪkt] 完美的
- **statue** [`stætʃuː]
  雕像；塑像
- **horrible** [`hɔːrəbl]
  可怕的；
  令人毛骨悚然的

p. 23

國王也發現到自己根本無法進食，
他對僕人咆哮道：
「我要回去找酒神！」
僕人四散準備動身，
但沒有人敢靠近國王。

- **realize** [`riːəlaɪz]
  領悟；了解
- **yell** [jel] 叫喊
- **run around** [rʌn ə`raund]
  四處奔走
- **prepare for**
  [prɪ`per fə(r)]
  為……準備

11

p. 24

隔天，國王跑進酒神的營帳中，
跪在酒神面前。
「請將這禮物收回！」
國王哀求道：
「這是件可怕的禮物！」
我害死了我的女兒！
而我自己也即將餓死！」
「那麼，好吧，你已經學到教訓了。」
酒神說：
「生命中有比財富更重要的東西。
你去帕克托樂斯河，
那裡有座噴泉，
你在噴泉裡將自己洗淨，
泉水會將這愚蠢的禮物帶走的。」

- **the next day**
  [ðə nekst deɪ] 隔天
- **threw oneself**
  [θru: wʌnˋself]
  將自己扔向……（threw
  是 throw 的過去式）
- **at . . . feet** [ət fi:t]
  在……的腳邊
- **starve to death**
  [stɑːrv tə deθ] 餓死
- **wealth** [welθ] 財富
- **the river Pactalus**
  帕克托樂斯河
- **spring** [sprɪŋ] 噴泉
- **take a bath** [teɪk ə bæθ]
  沐浴
- **take away** 帶走
- **foolish** [ˋfuːlɪʃ]
  愚蠢的；傻的

p. 25

〔圖〕酒神戴歐尼修斯

p. 26

國王長途跋涉來到帕克托樂斯河，。
他一看到泉水，馬上跳入河中。
泉水將他點石成金的力量沖走，

- **as soon as** [əz suːn əz]
  一……就……
- **carry . . . away** 帶走
- **golden touch**
  [ˋɡoʊldən tʌtʃ]
  點石成金的力量

但這力量並非完全消失，
它流進了河水之中。
河川沿岸有許多沙子，
沙子都變成了黃金！

- **completely** [kəm`pli:tlɪ]
  完全地
- **disappear** [dɪsə`pɪr] 消失
- **along** [ə`lɔ:ŋ] 沿著

---

p. 27

這條河位於利底亞境內。
因為麥達斯國王的緣故，
利底亞變得富裕，
不但成為了古代最富有的國家，
也是最早使用金幣的地方。

- **Lydia** 利底亞
  （女子名，涵意：財富）
- **richest** [`rɪtʃɪst] 最富有的
- **ancient** [`eɪnʃənt] 古代的
- **gold coin** 金幣
- **be used as**
  [bi ju:zd əz]
  像……一樣的使用

---

p. 28

國王麥達斯回到皇宮，
但女兒無法死而復生，
國王感到懊悔難過，
他決定拋棄一切財富，遁入森林。
他追隨自然之神潘，
從此遠離皇宮和黃金。

- **return to** [rɪ`tɜ:rn tə] 變回
- **ashamed** [ə`ʃeɪmd]
  羞愧的；感到難為情的
- **forget about**
  [fər`get ə`baut] 忘記……
- **follower** [`fɑ:louə(r)]
  追隨著
- **Pan** [pæn] 潘
  （希神；牧羊神）

父子逃亡記

p. 30

戴達勒斯是個睿智之士。
他是希臘最聰明的發明家，
也是雅典皇室的一員。

戴達勒斯深以自己的發明爲榮，
他的姐姐要他教導外甥皮帝斯。
戴達勒斯傾囊相受，
教了他許多事情。
皮帝斯是個聰明的孩子，
很快地就學會了。

- **smartest** [ˈsmɑːrtɪst]
  最聰明的（smart聰明的；smarter更聰明的）
- **inventor** [ɪnˈventə(r)]
  發明者
- **royal family**
  [ˈrɔɪəl ˈfæməli] 王室成員
- **Athens** [ˈæθɪnz]
  雅典城（希臘首都）
- **be proud of**
  [bi: praud ʌv]
  以……爲榮
- **invention** [ɪnˈvenʃn] 發明
- **nephew** [ˈnefjuː] 外甥

p. 31

有一天，皮帝斯在海邊散步，
他發現一副魚骨，
便用金屬製造了一副魚骨。
皮帝斯發現這副金屬魚骨，
是一個鋸木的好工具。
鋸子，就這樣被發明了出來！

- **spine** [spaɪn] 脊柱
- **copy** [ˈkɑːpi] 副本
- **metal** [ˈmetl]
  金屬；合金
- **wood** [wʊd] 木頭
- **easily** [ˈiːzəli]
  輕易地；容易地
- **saw** [sɔː] 鋸子

接下來，皮帝斯又找來兩塊金屬，
將金屬的一端削尖，
將另一端接合起來，
這個工具能夠畫出正圓，
也就是現在所說的「圓規」。

- **sharp** [ʃɑːrp] 鋒利的
- **join** [dʒɔɪn] 連結
- **draw** [drɔː] 劃
- **perfect** [ˋpɜːrfɪkt] 完美的
- **compasses** [ˋkʌmpəsɪz] 圓規

---

p. 32

人們很喜歡皮帝斯的發明，
戴達勒斯因此心中嫉妒。
有一天，
戴達勒斯喚來皮帝斯：
「皮帝斯，今天我要對你解釋『風』。」
他們爬到雅典衛城的上面，
戴達勒斯要外甥走到邊緣處，
「那裡是風力最強的地方。」
戴達勒斯解釋道。
皮帝斯來到邊緣，
戴達勒斯卻將他推下！

- **become jealous of** [bɪˋkʌm ˋdʒeləs ʌv] 變得對……嫉妒
- **Acropolis** [əˋkrɑːpəlɪs] 雅典衛城 （有巴森農神殿）
- **edge** [edʒ] 邊緣
- **roof** [ruːf] 屋頂
- **push** [puʃ] 推

p. 33

皮帝斯從屋頂掉落。

智慧和聰明之女神雅典娜，

看見皮帝斯即將摔落地面，

她深感同情，

就將皮帝斯變成一隻鳥，

人們稱這種新的鳥爲鷓鴣鳥。

這種鳥從不在高處築巢，

這是因爲皮帝斯當時是被推落的，

所以這種鳥只在接近地面的地方築巢。

- **fall off** [fɔːl ɔːf]
  落下；墮落
- **Athena** [ə`θinɑ] 雅典娜
- **wisdom** [`wɪzdəm] 智慧
- **intelligence**
  [ɪn`telɪdʒəns]
  智能；理解力
- **feel sorry for**
  爲……感到難過；同情
- **partridge** [`pɑːrtrɪdʒ]
  鷓鴣鳥
- **nest** [nest] 巢；窩
- **remember** [rɪ`membə(r)]
  紀念
- **ground** [graʊnd] 地面

p. 34

戴達勒斯難逃法網，

有人目睹他將皮帝斯推落屋頂。

鎮民審判他。

但由於他是皇室成員，

所以未被判死刑。

鎮民要他離開，永遠不得回來。

- **escape** [ɪ`skeɪp]
  逃避；逃離
- **punishment** [`pʌnɪʃmənt]
  懲罰
- **townsfolk** [`taʊnzfoʊk]
  城民；市民
- **judge** [dʒʌdʒ] 判決
- **instead** [ɪn`sted]
  作爲替代

戴達勒斯來到克里特島，
那裡的國王是麥諾斯。
戴達勒斯名聲遠播，
國王也對他略知一二。
國王便馬上雇用戴達勒斯，
要他為自己建造一座巨型迷宮。
國王想要將牛頭怪米諾托爾
關在迷宮中。
每九年，雅典人會送來十四個人，
供怪物食用。

- **hire** [ˈhaɪə(r)] 雇用
- **immediately** [ɪˈmiːdɪətli]
  立即地；馬上地
- **the Labyrinth**
  [ðə ˈlæbərɪnθ]
  拉比林特斯迷宮

p. 35
一年，
雅典英雄鐵修斯除掉了牛頭怪。
麥諾斯國王的女兒亞莉阿德妮，
愛上鐵修斯。
她將一團線球給了鐵修斯，
幫助他能輕易地走出迷宮。
鐵修斯進入迷宮，殺死牛頭怪，
然後與亞莉阿德妮一起逃離克里特島。
〔圖〕鐵修斯與亞莉阿德妮

- **Minotaur** 人身牛頭怪
- **fall in love with**
  [fɔːl ɪn lʌv wɪθ]
  愛上……；
  與……墜入愛河

17

p. 36

麥諾斯國王為此氣憤不已，
以為是戴達勒斯幫助鐵修斯脫逃的，
便將這位迷宮建造者及其子伊卡魯斯，
一起囚禁在高塔上。
戴達勒斯可以輕易逃離高塔，
卻不知道該如何逃離克里特島。
國王的將士守衛著所有船隻，
任何人想離開該島，
都會經過仔細搜身。

- **thought** [θɔːt] 思考；想
  （think 的過去式）
- **inventor** [ɪnˋventə(r)]
  發明者
- **get off** [get ɔːf]
  從……下來；離開
- **guard** [gɑːrd]
  守衛；保衛
- **left** [left] 離開
  （leave 的過去式）
- **search** [sɜːrtʃ] 搜查

p. 37

這天，戴達勒斯想了個好方法。
「國王麥諾斯掌控陸地與海洋，」
他心中想著：
「但他卻無法掌控天空，
所以我們可以從空中逃脫。」
戴達勒斯想了個聰明辦法，
他可以製作兩副翅膀，
一副給自己，一副給兒子，

- **have a good idea**
  [həv ə gʊd aɪˋdiːə]
  有個好辦法
- **control** [kənˋtroʊl] 控制
- **clever** [ˋklevə(r)] 聰明的
- **pair** [per] 一雙；一對
- **wing** [wɪŋ] 翅膀
- **set** [set]
- **Sicily** 西西里島

這樣他們就可以以飛離克里特島了！

戴達勒斯計畫飛到西西里島。
該地的國王很賢明，
他們不必再受麥諾斯國王的威脅。

----

p. 38

因此，戴達勒斯開始製作翅膀。
他收集禽鳥羽毛，
從蠟燭取來蠟液，
用線將羽毛綁在一起，
並用蠟液將小支羽毛黏著固定，
日夜不停地趕工。
有時，伊卡魯斯也幫父親收集羽毛。

- **collect** [kə`lekt] 收集
- **feather** [ˋfeðə(r)] 羽毛
- **wax** [wæks] 蠟
- **thread** [θred] 線
- **sometimes** [ˋsʌmtaɪmz] 有時候

19

p. 39

終於，戴達勒斯完成一副巨大的翅膀。
在著手為兒子製作第二副翅膀以前，
他必須先加以測試。
他將翅膀綁在自己手上，
接著上下快速地揮動雙臂，
他飛上天了！
快速揮動雙手，便能飛上天。
奮力展開雙手，便能慢慢降落。
這雙翅膀的確有用！
戴達勒斯很快製造另一副翅膀。

- **finally** [ˈfaɪnəli]
  最後；終於
- **test** [test] 測試
- **wave** [weɪv] 揮舞
- **flew** [flu] 飛行
  （flew 是 fly 的過去式）
- **spread** [spred]
  使伸展；使延伸
- **wide** [waɪd] 張得很大的
- **work** [wɜːrk]
  成功的；奏效的

p. 40

一天，天氣晴朗，
這是逃脫的時機。
戴達勒斯為兒子戴上翅膀，
自己也穿上。
他告誡伊卡魯斯要小心。
他說：「兒子，要緊跟著我，
不要飛得太低！
靠近海面的空氣比較濕，
會讓翅膀變重。」

- **clear** [klɪr] 晴朗的
- **put on** [pʊt ɑːn]
  戴上；裝上
- **own** [oʊn] 自己的
- **careful** [ˈkerfl] 小心的
- **dear** [dɪr] 親愛的
- **stay** [steɪ] 待在；停留在
- **too low** [tuː loʊ] 太低
- **in the air** [ɪn ði er]
  在空中
- **too heavy** [tuː ˈhevi] 太重

p. 41

「但也別飛得太高！
太陽會融化蠟液，
讓小羽毛脫落，
讓人摔下來。
要在海天之間比較涼爽乾燥的地方飛，
我會保持這個高度飛翔。
要緊跟著我！咱們飛吧！」
戴達勒斯邊說，邊揮動雙臂。
他知道飛翔是有危險性的。

- **melt** [melt] 融化
- **fall off** [fɔːl ɔːf]
  落下；跌下
- **in the cool, dry air**
  [ɪn ðə kuːl draɪ er]
  在涼爽乾燥的空氣中
- **flying** [ˈflaɪɪŋ] 飛行
- **dangerous** [ˈdeɪndʒərəs]
  危險的
- **shook** [ʃʊk] 搖動
  （shake 的過去式）

---

p. 42

戴達勒斯測試風向，
接著用力揮動雙臂，
便升到了空中。
他對伊卡魯斯大喊：
「跟著我，兒子！」
伊卡魯斯非常興奮，
隨即跟著父親。
他躍入空中，揮動雙臂，
飛了起來！
父子兩人一起飛離高塔。

- **rose** [rouz] 上升；升起
  （rise的過去式）
- **shout** [ʃaut] 呼喊；呼叫
- **back** [bæk] 後面的
- **follow** [ˈfɑːlou]
  跟隨；跟著
- **excited** [ɪkˈsaɪtɪd]
  興奮的

p. 43

起先航程一切順利，
西西里島在西邊遠處，
戴達勒斯看見太陽在東邊升起，
便遠離太陽。
沒多久，
他們就飛越了迪洛斯島和撒莫斯島，
戴達勒斯經常回頭看看兒子。
他們繼續飛往西邊，
但是太陽已經是日正當中，
戴達勒斯無法避開太陽，
因此他仔細觀察海洋和島嶼。

- **flight** [flaɪt] 飛行
- **well** [wel] 成功地；
  令人滿意地
- **far** [fɑːr] 遠遠的
- **pass** [pæs] 經過
- **check on** [tʃek ɑːn] 檢查
- **often** [ˋɔːfn] 時常；常常
- **no longer** [noʊ ˋlɔːnər]
  再不久；再不遠
- **closely** [ˋkloʊsli] 接近地

p. 44

伊卡魯斯覺得這樣飛很好玩！
他時而看著下面遠處的海浪，
時而看著海豚跳躍，
時而看到巨龜露出水面呼吸空氣，
等他看膩了海景，
他就抬頭看雲朵，
感覺雲就近在咫尺。

- **wave** [meɪv] 波浪
- **far** [fɑː(r)] 遠的
- **turtle** [ˋtɜːrtl] 烏龜
- **become tired of**
  [bɪˋkʌm ˋtaɪərd ʌv]
  變得對……感到疲倦
- **look down**
  [lʊk daʊn] 往下看
- **look up** [lʊk ʌp] 往上看
- **seem** [siːm]
  似乎；看來好像

p. 45

伊卡魯斯想飛入雲霄，
雲的形狀千奇萬化！
沒多久，他就越飛越高。
他飛向左、飛向右，
完全忘記父親的叮嚀。
在雲朵裡，又冷又暗，
因此他就飛上雲端，
雲端上的陽光很溫暖。

- **forgot** [fərˋgɑːt] 忘記
  （forget的過去式）
- **warning** [ˋwɔːrnɪŋ]
  警告；告誡
- **above** [əˋbʌv]
  在……上面

p. 46

太陽開始融化他翅膀上的蠟，

但他並未察覺，

還是越飛越高。

他喜歡太陽的溫暖。

沒多久，翅膀上的蠟都融化了。

羽毛開始從翅膀上掉落。

- **start to** [stɑ:t tə]
  開始去……
- **melt** [melt] 熔化
- **notice** [ˋnoʊtɪs] 注意
- **warmth** [wɔ:rmθ] 溫暖
- **soon** [su:n] 不久；
  很快地
- **fall from** [fɔl frʌm]
  從……落下

---

p. 47

伊卡魯斯突然才驚覺害怕，

但一切為時已晚，

翅膀開始出現破洞，

伊卡魯斯開始墜落，

他奮力揮動雙臂，

但仍舊往下掉落。

他更加用力揮臂，卻無濟於事，

只是直直往下掉落！

他向父親呼救，隨即落入水中。

戴達勒斯沒注意到

兒子飛得太靠近太陽，

只聽見伊卡魯斯的呼救聲。

- **suddenly** [ˋsʌdənli]
  突然地
- **afraid** [əˋfreɪd]
  害怕的
- **hole** [hoʊl]
  洞；破洞
- **appear** [əˋpɪr]
  出現；顯露
- **even** [ˋi:vn]
  甚至
- **cry out** [kraɪ aʊt]
  叫喊
- **call out** [kɔ:l aʊt]
  （大聲）呼叫

24

p. 48

戴達勒斯轉身查看，
卻看不到兒子的蹤跡。
他四處張望，上下尋找，
還是找不到兒子。
戴達勒斯大聲喊著：
「伊卡魯斯，
你在那裡？你在那裡？」
但是沒有任何回應。

- **turn around**
  [tɜːrn əˋraʊnd]
  往回轉；掉頭
- **shout** [ʃaʊt] 呼喊

---

p. 49

突然，
戴達勒斯看見水面上飄浮著羽毛，
便合起翅膀，
如石頭般向下俯衝，
他潛入水中，
發現兒子的蹤影。
兒子沉在水底，
動也不動。

- **next to** [nekst tə]
  在……旁
- **dove** [doʊv]
  潛下
  （dive的過去式）
- **be not moving**
  [bi nɑːt ˋmuːvɪŋ]
  動也不動的

25

p. 50

附近有個小島，
父親抓住兒子，將他拉上岸。
但一切已經太遲，
伊卡魯斯已氣絕身亡，
戴達勒斯抱著兒子的屍體良久，
痛哭哀號。
最後，他將兒子埋葬在島上。

這個埋葬伊卡魯斯的小島，
後來稱為「伊卡利島」。
而他所墜落的海洋，
則稱為「伊卡利海」。

- **nearby** [ˋnɪəbaɪ]
  附近的
- **grab** [græb]
  抓取
- **pull** [pʊl]
  拉
- **bury** [ˋberi]
  埋葬；安葬
- **Icaria** [ˌɪkɑˋreə]
  伊卡利島
- **Icarian Sea**
  [ˌɪkɑˋreun si:] 伊卡利海

美夢成真
——皮葛馬連與葛拉蒂

p. 52

皮葛馬連是一位技藝精湛的藝術家，
他住在塞普魯斯島上，
擅長雕琢精美塑像。
皮葛馬連樂於創作，
可以整天雕塑岩石與木頭。
他忙於創作，
無暇交遊。

- **Cyprus** 塞普魯斯
- **would** [wʊd] 將
- **spend** [spend]
  花費（時間）
- **shape** [ʃeɪp]
  形狀；外形

----

p. 53

他的父母希望他能成親。
他一表人才，才華出眾，
想要找到終身伴侶，
並非難事。
但皮葛馬連卻認為，
塞普魯斯島上的女人都很愚昧無知，
所以就發誓終身不娶，
整天沈醉在工作中，
他雕塑男人、女人、小孩和動物，
他最愛用的創作材料是象牙。

- **silly** [ˈsɪli] 愚昧無知
- **promise oneself**
  [ˈprɑːmɪs wʌnˈself]
  承諾自己
- **favorite** [ˈfeɪvərɪt]
  最喜愛的
- **material** [məˈtɪriəl]
  材料；原料
- **ivory** [ˈaɪvəri] 象牙

p. 54

一日，他見到一塊巨大象牙，
就把它買回家，
他花了好幾天來雕塑它，
有時甚至通宵工作。

終於，一座美麗的雕像完成了。
這是一座女人雕像，
是他最完美的作品。
這座雕像讓他聞名四海，
雕像栩栩如生，
幾乎就像活生生的女子一樣！
但女人們不喜歡這座雕像，
因爲雕像美得讓她們嫉妒。

雕像的膚色潔白，
美若仙子，
皮葛馬非常引以爲傲。

- **bought** [bɔːt] 買下
  （buy 的過去式）
- **all night** [ɔːl naɪt] 整晚
- **create** [krɪˋeɪt] 創造
- **best** [best] 最好的
- **ever** [ˋevə(r)]
  從來；至今
- **famous** [ˋfeɪməs]
  著名的；出名的
- **jealous** [ˋdʒeləs] 妒忌的
- **perfect** [ˋpɜːrfɪkt]
  完美的；理想的
- **be proud of**
  [bi praʊd ʌv]
  爲……感到驕傲的

p. 55

他會花上好幾個鐘頭，
痴痴看著雕像，
摸摸雕像的手臂或臉龐，
時而連自己都無法相信，
這竟會只是一座雕像，
而不是一個活生生的女子！
〔圖〕葛拉蒂雕像

- **put . . . on . . .**
  將……放置……上
- **believe** [bɪˋliːv] 相信
- **real** [ˋrɪəl]
  真的；真實的

---

p. 56

不久，
皮葛馬連的思緒全都被雕像佔滿，
他愛上雕像了！
他為雕像取了個名字，
稱她為「葛拉蒂」，
這是希臘文「睡美人」的意思。
他用象牙雕刻出小鳥和花朵，
放在葛拉蒂的腳旁。
他也為雕像製作項鍊，
將指環套在她的手指上，
甚至還為雕像穿上衣裳！
〔圖〕皮葛馬連與葛拉蒂

- **statue** [ˋstætʃuː] 雕像
- **fall in love** [fɔːl ɪn lʌv]
  愛上……
- **Greek** [griːk] 希臘
- **love** [lʌv] 愛；寶貝
- **out of** [aut ʌv]
  在……之外
- **necklace** [ˋneklǝs] 項鍊
- **ring** [rɪŋ] 戒指
- **even** [ˋiːvn] 甚至
- **clothes** [kloʊz]
  衣服；服飾

29

p. 57

夜晚時，
他會將葛拉蒂放在床上，
在她頭下放上柔軟的枕頭。
睡覺之前，他會親吻雕像。
她的肌膚看起來就像真人一樣，
白晰中透著紅潤血色。
然而，雕像摸起來仍是冰冷堅硬的，
畢竟，這只是一座象牙雕像。

- **pillow** [ˋpɪloʊ] 枕頭
- **kiss** [kɪs] 吻
- **pale** [peɪl] 白晰的
- **glow** [gloʊ] 光輝
- **touch** [tʌtʃ] 觸碰
- **after all** [ˋæftə(r) ɔːl]
  畢竟

---

p. 58

每年，在塞普魯斯有個嘉年華會。
這是為了愛與美之女神阿芙柔黛蒂
所舉辦的華會。
信眾來到她的神廟，
為女神獻上禮物，
祈禱自己能夠找到真愛。

皮葛馬連敬愛阿芙柔黛蒂，
他每年都會來到她的神廟，
為女神獻上許多精緻的小雕像。

- **festival** [ˋfestɪvl]
  節日；節慶
- **give** [gɪv] 賜予
- **pray** [preɪ] 祈禱；祈求
- **temple** [ˋtempl]
  神殿；聖堂
- **brought** [brɔːt]
  帶來
  （bring的過去式）

p. 59

今年，他一往如常來祭祀女神，
只不過，他這次的祈禱已有所不同。
他說著：「偉大的愛神，
請聆聽我的祈禱，
神是萬能的，
請賜給我一個妻子。」
他其實想說：
「請讓葛拉蒂成為吾妻。」
但他不敢如此無禮地要求，便說：
「請賜給我一位
長得像葛拉蒂的女子為妻。」

- **same** [seIm] 相同的
- **prayer** [prer]
  祈禱
- **hear** [hIr] 聽見
- **bold** [bould]
  放肆的；厚顏無恥的

p. 60

愛神聽到他的祈禱，
對他的禱詞印象深刻，
那聽起來非常的真誠熱切。

就在皮葛馬連禱告之際，
阿芙柔黛蒂來到皮葛馬連家中。
她看見床上葛拉蒂的象牙雕像，
也很驚訝雕像看起來
簡直就像真人一樣。

- **be impressed**
  [bi Im`prest]
  給……極深的印象；
  受感動的
- **sincere** [sIn`sIr] 誠懇的
- **while** [waIl] 當……
- **be amazed**
  [bi ə`meIzd] 吃驚的

p. 61

在神廟中，皮葛馬連仍在祈禱。
突然，蠟燭的火焰越燒越旺，
隨即變小。
皮葛馬連很驚訝。
之後火焰又變大了兩次。
神廟中的信眾紛紛感到驚喜。
這是女神應允祈禱的徵兆！
皮葛馬連也興奮不已，
心中升起一股好預兆，
於是連忙趕回家。

- **flame** [fleɪm]
  火焰；火舌
- **candle** [ˋkændl] 蠟燭
- **grew bigger**
  [gru: ˋbɪɡə(r)] 漸漸變大
  （grew 是 grow 的過去
  式）
- **feeling** [ˋfi:lɪŋ] 感覺
- **hurry** [ˋhɜ:ri] 趕緊

---

p. 62

夜晚，在睡覺之前，
他照例親吻葛拉蒂。
但，這是怎麼一回事？
葛拉蒂的雙唇不再冰冷僵硬，
而是變得柔軟而溫熱！
他將頭靠在雕像的手臂上，
這簡直令人難以置信！
肌膚竟是溫熱的！
肌膚底下是活絡絡的血管！

- **as usual** [əz ˋju:ʒuəl]
  一如往常
- **lip** [lɪp] 唇
- **soft** [sɔ:ft]
  柔軟的
- **warm** [wɔ:m]
  溫暖的
- **blood** [blʌd] 血液
- **softly** [ˋsɔ:ftli] 柔軟地

一開始，他驚訝得說不出話來，

接著他輕聲說道：

「謝謝妳，阿芙柔黛蒂，謝謝。」

p. 63

皮葛馬連再次親吻雕像，

不，現在這已不是一座雕像，

她的雙唇如此紅潤，

她睜開一雙深藍色的眼睛，

葛拉蒂變成真人了！

當葛拉蒂一張開雙眼，

她便愛上了皮葛馬連。

兩人開始籌畫婚禮。

- **ruby** [ˋruːbi] 紅寶石
- **deep** [diːp] 深深的
- **alive** [əˋlaɪv] 活著的
- **make plans for**
  [meɪk plæns fə(r)]
  替……做計劃

33

p. 64

阿芙柔黛蒂在神廟中，
為皮葛馬連與葛拉蒂證婚。

兩人感謝愛與美之女神
每年，
他們會在神廟中獻上許多禮物，
阿芙柔黛蒂也賜給他們永遠幸福的
婚姻生活。
皮葛馬連和葛拉蒂育有二女，
名為巴佛絲與美達米。

塞普魯斯的新城市，
便以巴佛絲命名，
這是敬拜阿芙柔黛蒂的主要地點。

- **in return** [ɪn rɪ`tɜːrn]
  以表回報
- **name after**
  [neɪm `æftə(r)]
  取名為
- **center** [`sentə(r)] 中心
- **honor** [`ɑːnər]
  為……增光

閱讀測驗

閱讀下列問題並選出最適當的答案。 ➜ 66-73 頁

▲點石成金的麥達斯

1. 麥達斯國王犯下了什麼錯？
   (A) 他喜愛黃金更勝於他的家人。
   (B) 他吃的太多，變得太胖。
   (C) 他在說話前不經思考。
   (D) 他沒有兒子。　　　　　答案 (C)

2. 席萊納斯和戴歐尼修斯之間的關係是？
   (A) 席萊納斯曾是戴歐尼修斯的老師。
   (B) 席萊納斯是戴歐尼修斯的父親。
   (C) 戴歐尼修斯是牧神之一。
   (D) 戴歐尼修斯是席萊納斯的叔叔。　　答案 (A)

3. 第一個被麥達斯國王變成黃金的是什麼東西？
   (A) 一顆蘋果。
   (B) 一段樹枝。
   (C) 一粒石頭。
   (D) 他種的玫瑰。　　　　　答案 (B)

4. 麥達斯國王把女兒變成黃金之後，對戴歐尼修斯說了什麼？

    (A) 酒神啊，請你不要生氣。

    (B) 我希望我碰過的東西都變成黃金。

    (C) 請把賜予我的能力收回吧。

    (D) 人生中還有更多比財富更重要的事。

答案 (C)

5. 麥達斯國王在哪裡擺脫掉他的能力？

    (A) 他的玫瑰花園。

    (B) 帕克托樂斯河。

    (C) 利底亞國境。

    (D) 森林中。

答案 (B)

6. 麥達斯國王在噴泉中做什麼？

    (A) 洗頭髮。

    (B) 游泳。

    (C) 喝水。

    (D) 洗澡。

答案 (D)

1. 戴達勒斯和皮帝斯兩人的關係為何？
   (A) 叔叔與外甥。
   (B) 父親與兒子。
   (C) 兄弟。
   (D) 主人與奴隸。

   答案 (A)

2. 誰發明了鋸子？

   答案 Perdix 皮帝斯

3. 皮帝斯所變成的鳥叫什麼名字？

   答案 partridge 鷓鴣鳥

4. 為什麼戴達勒斯要離開雅典娜城？
   (A) 因為他想要為麥諾斯國王工作。
   (B) 因為他想要逃到西西里島，在那裡他才是安全的。
   (C) 因為他殺害皮帝斯，被判有罪。
   (D) 因為他的家在西西里島。

   答案 (C)

5. 麥諾斯國王爲什麼要囚禁戴達勒斯和伊卡魯斯？

    (A) 因爲他對雅典城的人民感到生氣。

    (B) 因爲他以爲戴達勒斯曾經幫助一個從雅典城來
        的英雄。

    (C) 因爲他以爲戴達勒斯殺了牛頭怪。

    (D) 因爲他痛恨戴達勒斯和伊卡魯斯。

答案 (B)

6. 請選出下面戴達勒斯製作翅膀時所用上的材料。

    (A) 膠水。

    (B) 臘液。

    (C) 鳥的羽毛。

    (D) 衣服。

答案 (B), (C)

7. 伊卡魯斯是怎麼死的？

答案 Icarus flew too high and his wings fell apart. So he fell into the ocean.

伊卡魯斯飛得太高了，他的翅膀四散，所以就掉進海裡頭了。

38

1. 皮葛馬連以什麼維生？

   答案 He was a sculptor.

   他是個雕刻家。
   ----

2. 請選擇正確（T）或錯誤（F）。

   _____ 皮葛馬連不喜歡女人，因為她們都不漂亮。

   答案 False(F)

   _____ 阿芙柔黛蒂為皮葛馬連與葛拉蒂證婚。

   答案 True(T)

3. 葛拉蒂是什麼材料製成的？

   (A) 木頭。
   (B) 大理石。
   (C) 象牙。
   (D) 血肉和骨頭。

   答案 (C)

4. 阿芙柔黛蒂如何回應皮葛馬連的祈求？

   (A) 她透過神諭來告訴他未來的事。
   (B) 她託夢給他。
   (C) 她在她的神殿中以三次大火焰表示。
   (D) 她叫人帶訊息給他。

   答案 (C)

※閱讀下段文章，並討論之以下的問題。

……沒多久，兩人一起進入酒神的營帳裡。

酒神見到恩師，非常高興，

並問道：「老朋友，你去哪了呢？我們到處在找你呀，

後來我們聽說你在國王麥達斯那裡。

告訴我，恩師，國王待你如何？」

席萊納斯笑著回答：「他待我如皇親國戚呢，主子。

他用山珍海味款待我，我們大吃大喝，

歌唱讚美你。」

戴歐尼修斯想報答麥達斯國王，便說：

「敬愛的國王，你真是心胸寬大，我想送你一件禮物，

將你心中的願望告訴我，我將盡力滿足你。」……

1. 戴歐尼修斯賜予麥達斯國王「點石成金」的能力，
   但這對麥達斯國王來說，卻變成了一種詛咒。如果
   你是麥達斯，你會許下什麼願望呢？

   參考答案

   I would have wished for eternal life.

   我希望永生不死。

40

……伊卡魯斯覺得這樣飛很好玩！

他時而看著下面遠處的海浪，時而看著海豚跳躍，

時而看到巨龜露出水面呼吸空氣。等他看膩了海景，

他就抬頭看雲朵，感覺雲就近在咫尺。

伊卡魯斯想飛入雲霄，雲的形狀千奇萬化！

沒多久，他就越飛越高。

他飛向左、飛向右，完全忘記父親的叮嚀。

在雲朵裡，又冷又暗，因此他就飛上雲端，

雲端上的陽光很溫暖。……

2. 如果你像伊卡魯斯一樣能飛翔的話，你會想看什麼？

參考答案

I would want to look at the beautiful mountains of
Europe and to fly to the peak, and explore the valleys.

我會想要看看歐洲的美麗山岳，飛上山頭，然後在
山谷小溪間逛逛。

……不久，皮葛馬連的思緒全都被雕像佔滿，他愛上雕像了！

他為雕像取了個名字，稱她為「葛拉蒂」，這是希臘文「睡美人」的意思。

他用象牙雕刻出小鳥和花朵，放在葛拉蒂的腳旁。

他也為雕像製作項鍊，將指環套在她的手指上，甚至還為雕像穿上衣裳！

夜晚時，他會將葛拉蒂放在床上，在她頭下放上柔軟的枕頭。

睡覺之前，他會親吻雕像。她的肌膚看起來就像真人一樣，白晰中透著紅潤血色。……

3. 如果你是皮葛馬連的話，你還會爲葛拉蒂做些什麼，或做什麼送給她？

參考答案

I would have made a special room in my house just for Galatea.

我會在我的家中爲葛拉蒂打造一間專屬於她的房間。

42

黃道十二宮

黃道十二宮 → 64~68 頁

　　「黃道帶」（zodiac）這個字源自希臘文，意指「動物的環狀軌道」。黃道帶的起源為何？在本篇裡，你將可以看到說明星座來源的希臘神話故事：

　　太陽（the Sun）、地球（the Earth）、牡羊座（the Ram）、金牛座（the Bull）、雙子座（the Twins）、巨蟹座（the Crab）、獅子座（the Lion）、處女座（the Virgin）、天秤座（the Balance）、天蠍座（the Scorpion）、射手座（the Archer）、摩羯座（the Goat）、寶瓶座（the Water Bearer）、雙魚座（the Fishes）。

> 1. Aries（the Ram）牡羊座
> 2. Libra（the Balance）天秤座
> 3. Taurus（the Bull）金牛座
> 4. Scorpio（the Scorpion）天蠍座
> 5. Gemini（the Twins）雙子座
> 6. Sagittarius（the Archer）射手座
> 7. Cancer（the Crab）巨蟹座
> 8. Capricorn（the Goat）摩羯座
> 9. Leo（The Lion）獅子座
> 10. Aquarius（the Water Bearer）寶瓶座
> 11. Virgo（the Virgin）處女座
> 12. Pisces（the Fishes）雙魚座

牡羊座（the Ram） 3.21-4.20

牡羊座源自於金羊毛的故事。白羊安全營救福里瑟斯，福里瑟斯把金羊獻祭給宙斯作為回報，宙斯便將金羊形象化為天上星座。

金牛座（the Bull） 4.21-5.20

金牛座源自於歐羅巴和公牛的故事。宙斯化身為公牛，以便吸引歐羅巴，公牛載著歐羅巴跨海來到克里特島。宙斯將公牛的形象化為星座，以為紀念。

雙子座（the Twins） 5.21-6.21

雙子座源自於卡斯特與波樂克斯的故事。他們兩人為孿生兄弟，彼此相親相愛。為了紀念其兄弟情誼，宙斯將他們的形象化為星座。

巨蟹座（the Crab）　6.22-7.22

巨蟹座源自於赫丘力的十二項苦差役。希拉派遣巨蟹前去殺害赫丘力，但是赫丘力在打敗九頭蛇之前，一腳將巨蟹踩碎。為了紀念巨蟹，希拉將其形象化為星座。

獅子座（The Lion）　7.23-8.22

獅子座亦源自於赫丘力十二項苦差中。赫丘力的第一項苦差，是要殺死奈米亞山谷之獅。他徒手殺了獅子，為了紀念這項偉大的事蹟，宙斯將奈米亞獅子的形象，置於星辰之中。

處女座（the Virgin）　8.23-9.22

處女座源自於潘朵拉的故事。處女指的是純潔與天真女神阿絲蒂雅。潘朵拉好奇將禁盒打開，讓許多邪惡事物來到人間，眾神紛紛返回天庭。為了紀念這種失落的純真，便把阿絲蒂雅的形象置於群星中。

天秤座（the Balance） 9.23-10.21

天秤是正義的秤子，由神聖正義女神蒂米絲隨身攜帶。天秤座落在處女座旁邊，因為阿絲蒂雅是蒂米絲之女。

天蠍座（the Scorpion） 10.22-11.21

天蠍座源自於歐里昂。歐里昂和阿蒂蜜絲是一對狩獵夥伴，阿蒂蜜絲的哥哥阿波羅對此忌妒不已。他請求蓋亞殺了歐里昂。因此，蓋亞創造天蠍殺了偉大的歐里昂。為了紀念此事，宙斯將歐里昂和天蠍化成星座。這兩個星座從來不會同時出現。

射手座（the Archer） 11.23-12.21

射手座代表卡隆。在希臘神話故事中，卡隆是許多英雄的朋友，例如亞吉力、赫丘力。赫丘力以毒箭誤傷了卡隆。卡隆是神，因此得以不死，但是卻必須忍受這無止盡的痛苦，所以卡隆央求宙斯殺了他。為了紀念卡隆，宙斯將他化為星座。

摩羯座（the Goat）　12.22-1.19

魔羯代表哺育年幼宙斯的羊阿瑪爾夏。
據說宙斯為了感念此羊，將之化為星座。

寶瓶座（the Water Bearer）　1.20-2.18

寶瓶座源自於鐸卡連的洪水。在這個故事中，宙
斯在人間降下豪雨，讓洪水沖走一切邪惡的生
物。只有鐸卡連和妻子皮雅是洪水的生還者。

雙魚座（the Fishes）　2.19-3.20

雙魚座代表愛與美之女神阿芙柔黛蒂，
以及其子愛神愛羅斯。當時有個颱風，
兩人沿著優芙瑞特河步行。他們請求宙
斯援救，宙斯將兩人變成魚，讓他們安
然渡過風災。為了紀念此事，阿芙柔黛
蒂化身為星座中的大魚，愛羅斯則化為
小魚。

故事原著作者 Thomas Bulfinch

Without a knowledge of mythology much of the elegant literature of our own language cannot be understood and appreciated.

缺少了神話知識，就無法了解和透徹語言的文學之美。

—*Thomas Bulfinch*

Thomas Bulfinch（1796-1867），出生於美國麻薩諸塞州的Newton，隨後全家移居波士頓，父親為知名的建築師Charles Bulfinch。他在求學時期，曾就讀過一些優異的名校，並於1814年畢業於哈佛。

畢業後，執過教鞭，爾後從商，但經濟狀況一直未能穩定。1837年，在銀行擔任一般職員，以此為終身職業。後來開始進一步鑽研古典文學，成為業餘作家，一生未婚。

1855年，時值59歲，出版了奠立其作家地位的名作*The Age of Fables*，書中蒐集希臘羅馬神話，廣受歡迎。此書後來與日後出版的 *The Age of Chivalry*（1858）和 *Legends of Charlemagne*（1863），合集更名為 *Bulfinch's Mythology*。

本系列書系，即改編自 *The Age of Fable*。Bulfinch 著寫本書時，特地以成年大眾為對象，以將古典文學引介給一般大眾。*The Age of Fable* 堪稱十九世紀的羅馬神話故事的重要代表著作，其中有很多故事來源，來自Bulfinch自己對奧維德（Ovid）的《變形記》（*Metamorphoses*）的翻譯。

■Bulfinch 的著作

1. Hebrew Lyrical History.
2. The Age of Fable: Or Stories of Gods and Heroes.
3. The Age of Chivalry.
4. The Boy Inventor: A Memoir of Matthew Edwards, Mathematical-Instrument Maker.
5. Legends of Charlemagne.
6. Poetry of the Age of Fable.
7. Shakespeare Adapted for Reading Classes.
8. Oregon and Eldorado.
9. Bulfinch's Mythology: Age of Fable, Age of Chivalry, Legends of Charlemagne.